For my dad, John Havlik,
who rarely enforced bath time
-S.M.

To Sidney and Ashley
-J.A.

Visit us on the Web! randomhousekids.com

Educators and librarians, for a variety of teaching tools, visit us at
RHTeachersLibrarians.com

Library of Congress Cataloging-in-Publication Data
Names: McAnulty, Stacy, author. | Ang, Joy, illustrator.
Title: 101 reasons why I'm not taking a bath / by Stacy McAnulty ;
illustrated by Joy Ang.
Other titles: One hundred and one reasons why I'm not taking a bath |
One hundred one reasons why I'm not taking a bath | 101 reasons why I am not taking a bath
Description: First edition. | New York : Random House, 2016. | Summary: A young boy
who thinks baths are dumb, dangerous, and a complete waste of time changes his mind
after finally getting into the tub with his toy boat.
Identifiers: LCCN 2015023380 | ISBN 978-0-385-39189-4 (hardcover) |
ISBN 978-0-375-97365-9 (hardcover library binding) | ISBN 978-0-385-39190-0 (ebook)
Subjects: | CYAC: Baths—Fiction. | Cleanliness—Fiction. | Humorous stories.
Classification: LCC PZ7.M47825255 Aam 2016 | DDC [E]—dc23

MANUFACTURED IN CHINA
10 9 8 7 6 5 4 3 2 1
First Edition

Book design by John Sazaklis

101 Reasons Why I'm NOT Taking a Bath

by **Stacy McAnulty**

illustrated by **Joy Ang**

RANDOM HOUSE 🏠 NEW YORK

Bath time?
No way.

Give you a reason?

I'll give you 101 reasons.

I'm not dirty.

I'm allergic to water.

To soap.

To shampoo.

To tile floors.

My sensitive skin needs blue soap,
   and you keep buying green soap.

Bubbles could get in my nose.

My mouth.

My eyes.

My ears.

My brain.

Baths are too **WET**!

And water makes my fingers wrinkly.

And my toes.

And my butt. (At least I think it does.)

I'm not as dirty as Sam,
   who lost when we played
   mud tag.

Or as Joe,
   who came in last
   when we rolled down
   Dandelion Hill.

Or Lee, who got
   stuck in the slime
   tunnel during the
   obstacle course.

And none of my friends
have to take baths.

I'll clean myself
like the cat.

The dog only takes a
bath like twice a year.

I think I could fit
in this birdbath.

I'll rinse off in that puddle.

You should clean the car instead—I don't have bird poop on me.

The sprinkler would be faster.

But I don't smell
as bad as this.

Or this.

ROSES

Or this.

Or this.

Aliens might attack
   while I'm in the bath.

Or there might be
   a meteor shower.

Or the sun might burn out.

Or a comet might crash
   into our neighborhood.

Or the moon might fall
   out of orbit.

Besides, I can't find my arm floaties.

I need arm floaties.

And goggles.

And a scuba tank.

And a surfboard.

And a canoe.

Fine! I just need my bike.

I can't take a bath on an empty stomach.

I need a cupcake.

Or a cookie.

Or a lollipop.

Just one lick of a *lollipop*?

Then can I have a carrot stick?

I need to wait thirty minutes after eating
  before I can get in the water.

I mean thirty hours.

I'll only take a bath in the sink.

Or in the dishwasher.

Look! I have
a self-cleaning
button like
the oven.

1
2
3
4
5
6
7
8
9
10
11
12
13
14
15
16
17
18
19
20
21
22
23
24
25
26
27
28
29
30

I took a bath yesterday. . . . Then it was
the day before. . . . Then it was the day
before the day before.

I'll take a bath tomorrow. I'll take three.
Five. Ten. That's my final offer.

I'm not dirty. That's a freckle.
And so is that.
And that's a whole town of freckles.

Hey, look! A clean spot.
I'll just clean up with hand sanitizer
and air freshener.

I haven't finished my puzzle.

Or my clay vase in the shape of a volcano.

Or my finger-paint portrait of the family.

Or my model of the White House
made of macaroni.

Or my drawing of our
house at night.

A bath won't help.

This is **permanent** marker.

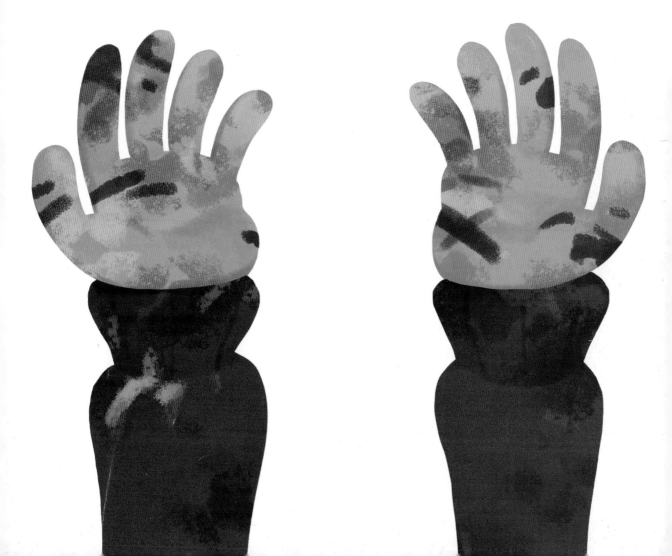

Most household accidents
happen in the bathroom.
Scientific fact!

Baths kill trees.
Scientific fact!

A kid in Texas turned into a
prune after taking a bath.
Scientific fact!

I'm not dirty.

This floor is dirty.

And this chimney.

And this coffee table.

Every time I turn around, I find
    something dirtier than me.

I don't understand why you want me to take a bath. It's not your birthday.

We're not going to be on TV. Are we?

The president isn't coming over.

I'll take a bath before I get married. . . . And I'm never getting married.

Please don't make me go in there.

Monsters live in the drain.
Slimy, hairy monsters.

The faucet gives me nightmares
  about waterfalls.

I've seen an invisible crocodile in the tub.
I mean, I've *heard* an invisible crocodile
  in the tub.

Ghosts haunt the soap dish.

Dragons live behind the towel rack.

Did you hear that?
I think it was lightning.

All the towels are dirty.

The dog ate the washcloths.

My rubber *Iguanodon* used all the shampoo
    to make his lagoon.

The soap ran away to Antarctica.

I'll be your best friend.

I'll give you my dessert—forever.

I'll clean your room. . . .

No, not *my* room. That's a mess.

I said *your* room.

Okay. Name your price.

And reason number 101 . . .

I'M NOT DIRTY!

What do you mean,
   I already used that one?

And what do you mean,
   that's only **88**?

You've actually been counting?

I don't want to. I don't want to. I don't want to.
I don't want to. I don't want to. I don't want to.
I don't want to. I don't want to. I don't want to.
I don't want to. I don't want to. I don't want to.
I don't want to.

Time to get out?

I'm not getting out.

And I'll give you
102 reasons why!